Fiona & Frieda's
Fairy-tale Adventures

Cinderella and the
Bowling Slipper

by Nadia Higgins   illustrated by Meredith Johnson

magic
wagon

visit us at www.abdopublishing.com

Published by Magic Wagon, a division of the ABDO Group, 8000 West 78th Street, Edina, Minnesota 55439. Copyright © 2009 by Abdo Consulting Group, Inc. International copyrights reserved in all countries. All rights reserved. No part of this book may be reproduced in any form without written permission from the publisher.

Calico Chapter Books™ is a trademark and logo of Magic Wagon.

Printed in the United States.

Text by Nadia Higgins
Illustrations by Meredith Johnson
Edited by Patricia Stockland
Interior layout and design by Rebecca Daum
Cover design by Rebecca Daum

Library of Congress Cataloging-in-Publication Data
Higgins, Nadia.
  Cinderella and the bowling slipper / by Nadia Higgins ; illustrated by Meredith Johnson.
      p. cm. — (Fiona & Frieda's fairy-tale adventures)
  ISBN 978-1-60270-572-2
  [1. Fairy tales—Fiction. 2. Characters in literature—Fiction.]
I. Johnson, Meredith, ill. II. Title.
  PZ7.H5349558Cin 2009
  [Fic]—dc22
                                                2008038261

For Lucie, the most fun—N. H.

Fiona

Frieda

Chapter 1

Once upon a time in a land not far away at all (actually just down the street from Moonlight Lanes Bowling Alley), there lived two third graders, Fiona and Frieda. Fiona and Frieda were best friends. They were neighbors, too. Fiona lived at 801 Castle Apartments, and Frieda lived at 802.

More than cake, more than fireworks, more than TV, and even more than Christmas, Fiona and Frieda loved fairy tales. Fiona owned 18 pairs of fairy wings, 42 magic wands, and 11 tiaras. Frieda owned 43 witch hats,

6 cauldrons, and one-and-a-half sets of pretend creepy nails.

Fiona and Frieda went to Sprinkledust Elementary School. Each day at recess the friends would meet under the curly blue slide.

"Who do you want to be?" Fiona would ask Frieda.

"Who do you want to be?" Frieda would ask Fiona.

Then the girls would act out fairy tales. Fiona was usually a princess, a fairy, or a mermaid. But, some days she was a fairy princess or a princess mermaid. Frieda was usually a witch or an evil queen, but she didn't mind playing the beast or the wolf. She'd also play the prince, if she really had to.

Fiona and Frieda called their game Fairy-tale Adventures. They played Fairy-tale Adventures every day of first grade. They played it every day of second grade. Then, on the fifty-seventh day of third grade, something amazing happened.

The girls started the game the way they always did. In her witchiest voice, Frieda began chanting a spell:

Eye of frog,
Enchanted hog,
Magic willow,
Flying pillow . . .

While Frieda chanted, Fiona danced around, waving her magic wand. The day before, she'd waved a pencil with an eraser shaped like kissy lips. Today, it was a cottony-tipped dandelion.

Well, it just so happened that Frieda was allergic to that fluffy white stuff. At one point, Fiona did a big, swoopy wave and—

"Aaaaah-aaaah-aaaaaah—"

Frieda froze. Eyes closed, mouth open, she was poised for an enormous sneeze.

So Fiona picked up the spell where Frieda left off. In her sweetest, good-witch voice, she continued:

A sneezing chum,
A stick of gum,
A grand to-do,
No boo-hoo—

Then, exactly as Fiona finished her rhyme, Frieda came back to life.

"Hoo," Fiona said.

"Choooo!" Frieda sneezed at the exact same moment.

Was it their spell? Was it the white fluff fluttering everywhere? All of a sudden, the air looked really weird, as if it were full of magic. Like that stuff that drips off a fairy's wand.

"What *was* that?" Frieda asked, rubbing her eyes.

Fiona didn't know, but she didn't want to break out of character with only ten minutes left of recess. She was playing a fairy princess, so she just went with it. She figured that whatever had happened could only make the game even greater.

"Oh, my poor child, are you quite alright?" she asked Frieda, waving her magic wand (now just the stem of a dandelion) over her head.

Sniff.

"Now, now, don't cry," Fiona said. She liked where the game was going.

Sniff. Hiccup. Oooooooooh.

"Frieda?" Fiona bent down to look at her friend. Frieda was really good at pretend crying, but she wasn't this good.

Whaaaaaa!

"Is that *you*, Fiona?" Frieda asked. The two girls looked at each other. Not a tear, not a smudge on either face.

"Huh?" Fiona said.

"Huh?" Frieda said.

They looked around. That's when things got really creepy. They could see all the other kids on the playground—swinging, chasing each other, playing dodgeball—*but the kids weren't making a single sound.* Everything was silent except for the girls' own voices and—

"What now? What am I going to do?"

There, sitting on the edge of the curly blue slide, was a real maiden. She wore a scratchy, brown dress with an apron over it. But she was still really beautiful. Her shiny, blonde hair was ribbony and soft, like cake frosting. And she had sparkly, blue eyes and a little pink mouth like a pencil eraser.

While the maiden was dripping tears all over the slide, she made circles in the sand with her feet. Her feet! They were as small as a second grader's.

"Cinderella?" Frieda whispered.

"Cinderella!" Fiona yelped.

The maiden didn't look up. She just kept tracing patterns with her feet. "Yes, it's me, Cinderella. Oh, Fairy Godmother? Is that you?"

Then, before Fiona and Frieda could figure

out what to say, Cinderella started gushing, "Oh, Fairy Godmother. I'm really in trouble now. Surely, you've heard about the ball at the king's castle? All the young maidens are to attend, and the prince is going to choose a wife. And it's *tonight*.

"Well, you see, when the king's messenger showed up with the invitation, my mean stepmother was outside planting weeds for me to pick. And my two mean stepsisters were in the kitchen sprinkling mold on my dinner. So I was the one who answered the door.

"There I was, all alone in the foyer, clutching that invitation. One thought ran through my head: *I must, must go.* But I knew my mean stepfamily would find a way to prevent me. Then it occurred to me: *What if . . . what if I just didn't tell them?* Everyone thinks I'm so sweet and kind. If I got rid of the invitation, nobody would ever, ever suspect me.

"So, I made a plan: I would make a dress in secret. Then on the night of the ball, I would pretend I was going outside to polish the garden ornaments. I would slip off to the ball, meet the prince, and live happily ever after. . . ."

Cinderella was so quiet for so long, Fiona couldn't stand it any longer.

"So . . . what went wrong?" she finally asked.

Chapter 2

Cinderella finally looked up at Fiona and Frieda.

"Oh, hello there," she said, wiping her nose with the back of her sleeve. "Sorry, I thought you were my Fairy Godmother. . . . Though I can't imagine why. She never appears when I need her."

"Really?" Frieda asked.

"Indeed," Cinderella continued. "For example, I sent her six notes asking her to meet me here—at the curly blue slide—and she never even wrote back. Still, I thought maybe—"

Cinderella's petal-pink lips started quivering.

"It's okay," Fiona said. She hugged Cinderella. "Maybe we can help you. My name is Fiona."

"And I'm Frieda."

"You can trust us," Fiona said.

"We know everything about fairy tales," Frieda added.

"We're fairy-tale experts!" Fiona said.

Cinderella smiled. "You're so very kind."

"Soooooo," Fiona said. "Tell us. You realized you could destroy the invitation. What happened next? Did you really destroy it?"

Fiona and Frieda squeezed in on either side of Cinderella.

"Well," Cinderella continued. "I decided to go forward with my plan, but I couldn't bear to destroy the invitation. It was so lovely, with bumpy cursive letters and ribbons, rose petals, and glitter everywhere. It inspired me. I painted a heart on it. Inside the heart, I wrote 'Cinderella + The Prince, TLA.' "

"TLA?" Frieda asked.

"True Love Always," Fiona explained.

Cinderella sighed a little. It looked as if she were studying a beautiful painting that was far away.

"Every day," she continued, "I collected ferns and silver feathers, rainbow light and sea foam, sparkling dew and shimmering webs—nature's most beautiful gifts. And each evening, I sewed them together into the most amazing dress."

"Ooooooh," Fiona said, looking at the dress in her imagination.

"Then—oh, what a mistake—," Cinderella continued. "One night I hid the invitation in a crack in the wall of my bedroom. Of course, the mice found it, and they used it to wallpaper their living room. And then—"

Cinderella's voice got all squeaky at the next part.

"That awful, evil, horrid cat stole it! The last time I saw him, he was batting it between his paws in my stepsisters' bedroom."

Cinderella shivered a little.

"The next thing I knew, my stepsisters were screaming my name. I could hear them clomping across the marble floors toward my room. . . . Well, I didn't wait for them to catch me. I started running and—"

"Cinderella! Cinderella!" two new voices— the squeakiest, crackliest, meanest voices ever— shrieked across the silent playground.

"It's them!" Cinderella gasped. "My stepsisters!"

"Come on—inside the yellow tubes!" Frieda said. Panting, the girls and the maiden crawled inside the nearby playground thingy.

The girls peeked through the tube's bubble window. There were the stepsisters, with their hair all curled up like springy sausages, their shiny, frilly dresses slithering in the sand behind them.

The stepsister with the straw-colored hair tripped over a red rubber ball. When she fell, she kicked up sand in her sister's face—the one with the fuzzy caterpillar eyebrows. The next thing you knew, the stepsisters were throwing sand in each other's faces.

"How did they find me?" Cinderella wondered aloud.

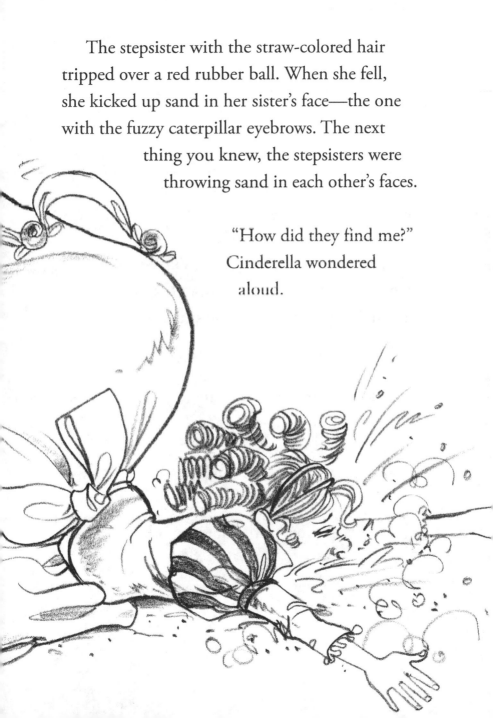

The stepsisters were wrestling under the jungle gym now. Sand was flying. Hair was flying. Shiny fabric was flying.

Frieda just sat there studying every detail, taking it all in. That's when she noticed something really important.

"One, two, three, four, five, six . . . ," she counted the neat, pink envelopes that had started flying, too. The whole situation was instantly clear to her.

"How many notes did you say you sent to the Fairy Godmother?" Frieda asked Cinderella.

"Uh, six," Cinderella said.

"And you wrote in the notes to have the Fairy Godmother meet you *here*?" Frieda continued.

"Yes—Oh!" Cinderella looked at the pink envelopes scattered on the ground. "My mean stepsisters stole my letters to my Fairy Godmother!"

Chapter 3

The stepsisters were brushing each other off now. They were back on the prowl for poor Cinderella.

Frieda was really on a roll, because just then she came up with another smart idea.

"What do the stepsisters hate more than anything else in the world?" Frieda asked Cinderella.

"That would definitely be chores of any kind," Cinderella said.

That's when Fiona caught on to Frieda's plan.

"To the custodian's closet!" Fiona said.

"Brilliant! They'd never go there!" Cinderella said.

Fiona, Frieda, and Cinderella waited for their chance. Soon, the stepsisters were fighting again. *Squeak. Squeak.* They were wrestling for a turn on the squeaky swing.

"Let's go!"

The three girls took off toward the school. It was amazing how fast Cinderella could run, with her tiny feet and all. (Luckily, she wasn't wearing her glass slippers.)

The girls ran inside the school. They hid behind the door just as Mr. Shinefloor, the school custodian, was walking outside. He was muttering to himself and heading toward the squeaky swing with an oilcan.

"That was close!" Fiona said, giggling and clapping her hands a little.

Frieda couldn't have clapped her hands even if she'd wanted to—which she certainly didn't. She was too busy chewing her fingernails like a crazy, fingernail-eating beaver.

"Come on, come on!" Frieda ordered. She led the group toward the brown metal door at the end of the corridor.

The custodian's closet was one of Fiona and Frieda's secret places. Even though it smelled like lemons and cough syrup, it was a place they counted on to be left alone. It was where they went to think—which was exactly what Fiona and Frieda needed to do.

The smell made Cinderella sick to her stomach. This was kind of weird, since she usually cleaned all day. Or maybe that was why.

Anyway, the girls and Cinderella sat on overturned buckets and thought and thought about what they should do. Fiona twirled her hair with a pencil. Cinderella hugged her stomach. Frieda kept saying over and over, "We need a plan, we need a plan." Suddenly Fiona stood up and shouted, "The Fairy Godmother!"

"Not her again," Cinderella groaned.

"But don't you see?" Fiona said. "She never got your letters. She probably doesn't even *know* you need her."

"Well, what kind of Fairy Godmother is *that*?" Cinderella asked. Given the godmother's whole "fairy" powers and all, Frieda had to admit that Cinderella had a point. Then again, Frieda

reasoned, anyone who's ever read the Cinderella fairy tale knows that the Fairy Godmother comes through in the end.

"It's worth a shot. Trust us," Frieda told Cinderella.

Frieda had already had two good ideas, so Cinderella smiled and agreed. She tried to hand Frieda a glittery blue slip of paper, but the paper floated away. Cinderella sighed, then she swatted at the thing like it was a fly.

"Here. Hold on to it," she said, handing the paper over. "It's the Fairy Godmother's business card."

Fiona and Frieda looked at the card. Frieda gasped. Fiona gasped.

This is what the card said:

Miranda Merryball
Fairy Godmother
Handling mean stepsisters for
more than 250 years

Call today at 555-KNAB-A-PRINCE

803 Castle Apartments

"You mean—," Fiona said.

"Are you serious?" Frieda said.

They looked at each other. Then Frieda giggled. Then Fiona giggled. Then Frieda snorted, and Fiona fell down laughing. "Mrs. Nuttyball is the Fairy Godmother!" Fiona shrieked.

Mrs. Merryball was Fiona and Frieda's wackiest neighbor on the eighth floor of Castle Apartments. She was such a nut job that everyone called her Mrs. Nuttyball. We're talking

Easter eggs for Halloween nutty. And a garden on her balcony where she only ever, ever grew zucchini nutty. And shoes made out of pistachio shells nutty. *That* nutty.

Cinderella was starting to look concerned. "Um, excuse me, is there a problem?"

"Problem?" Frieda said, wiping her eyes. "None at all. In fact, we know *exactly* where to find your Fairy Godmother."

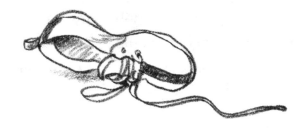

Chapter 4

So now all the girls had to do was figure out how to ditch the stepsisters and get out of the closet before Cinderella lost her lunch. Fiona only did a couple hair twirls before the greatest plan ever came to her.

"I'll be right back!" she said, pushing open the heavy, brown door.

"What? Wait!" Frieda called after her.

"No time to expla—!" Fiona called back.

Slam. Then, a second later, *creaaaak.*

When Fiona came back, she was carrying her
Snow White backpack.

"No offense," she said to Cinderella, but
Cinderella was too sick to even notice the
backpack's decorations. Then Fiona dug down
deep. First, she pulled out two bowling shirts.
The pink shirts had black collars
and black buttons and the
words *Sprinkledust Bowling
Club* written across the back
in black, fuzzy letters.
One shirt had *Fiona*
in cursive
letters
across
the

front pocket; the other one had *Frieda*. Next, Fiona pulled out two pairs of bowling shoes. This plan was so creative, even Frieda was not picking up on it.

"Huh?" Frieda said. "Bowling club's not until after school, Fiona. And why are you worried about that now? We've *got* to think of a way to get Cinderella safe!"

But Fiona was too busy to answer. "Here, Cinderella. You can be me." She handed Cinderella the Fiona shirt. "You put yours on, too, Frieda. It will add to the disguise."

"Of course, a disguise!" Frieda said. Everyone who's read *Cinderella* knows that even the stepsisters don't recognize Cinderella at the ball. And this was a much better disguise than just a gown and a tiara.

"Those mean stepsisters will never recognize

you in bowling shoes," Fiona said, as she unpinned and unrolled Cinderella's beautiful hair.

"No . . . ," Cinderella moaned as Fiona messed up her hair.

"Sorry," Fiona said. "But your hair is still way too fancy for bowling club."

When Fiona was done, Cinderella's hair hung in her eyes. Her skirt sprang out from under her bowling shirt and didn't match at all. And then there were the bowling shoes.

Cinderella looked—well, she looked like a wonderfully ordinary member of the Sprinkledust Bowling Club.

"Okay," Fiona said, looking at Cinderella with satisfaction. She peeked outside. "The coast is clear. I'll go get Mrs. Nutty, I mean

Mrs. Merryball. We'll meet you at Moonlight Lanes in 15 minutes."

Fiona was right. The stepsisters didn't recognize Cinderella in her bowling disguise. In fact, they walked right up to Cinderella and Frieda and asked them for directions. That made Frieda crazy! The stepsisters were two of her very favorite evil characters. And, she couldn't ask them a single question, like who's *their* favorite evil character.

Frieda and Cinderella got to Moonlight Lanes first. Cinderella's stomach was feeling much better. Only now she was getting nervous. The ball started in half an hour, and it would take her at least 45 minutes to go home and pick up her dress.

"Don't worry," Frieda said. "You're going to get to the ball. You have to get to the ball." Deep down though, she was starting to worry, too.

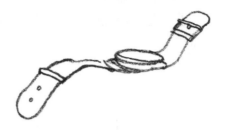

Chapter 5

Frieda did what she always did when she wanted to calm down. She made lists in her head. She listed all the names she knew that started with F. Then she listed frog species. Then she did all the things she loves about *The Wizard of Oz*. She'd just thought *flying monkeys* when—finally!—Fiona and Mrs. Merryball swept into the bowling alley.

Crunch. Crunch. Crunch.

Mrs. Merryball ran toward Cinderella in her pistachio-shell shoes. She was wearing some

Rules

loose, red wrap thing that fluttered when she moved. She looked like a giant butterfly running across the bowling alley.

"My poor, poor dear!" She swallowed up Cinderella in a big, flowery hug. "Fiona told me everything. Oh, my dear, my dear. I never got your letters, and—silly me—I got my years mixed up again and thought the ball was at least a year away—certainly not this year, certainly not *tonight*."

Cinderella managed to pop her head out of Mrs. Merryball's hug.

Mrs. Merryball looked down at the maiden. "Oh, my dear, my dear. What have they done to you?"

Frieda explained that it was all just a disguise—and a very good one, too, thanks to her friend, Fiona.

"Please, Fairy Godmother," Cinderella said, now free of the nutty lady's grip. "You have to help me. We have so little time."

At this Mrs. Merryball touched her toes. She stood up. She waved her arms and twirled them in the air. Fiona and Frieda looked at each other. Fiona made the "crazy" sign. She looked so funny that Frieda had to do two more lists in her head to keep from rolling on the floor laughing.

"Just loosening up the magic," Mrs. Merryball explained. "Now then," she looked around. "Hmmmmmm."

She pulled out her magic wand. "Row, row, row your boat, gently down the stream . . . ," she started to sing.

Frieda poked Fiona. "*That's* her magic song?" she whispered, snorting behind her hand.

But Fiona didn't even look at Frieda, because she knew she'd lose it.

Mrs. Merryball pointed her wand at a red, pearly-swirly bowling ball. *Poof!* The bowling ball turned into a red, pearly-swirly fairy-tale coach.

"Nice work!" Fiona said.

"How nice of you to notice," said Mrs. Merryball.

The Fairy Godmother lifted her wand again. "Merrily, merrily, merrily, merrily . . ." *Poof!* The guy behind the shoe rentals desk was now sitting on the coach, holding the horse's reigns.

"The coachman!" Fiona said.

"Too itchy! Too itchy!" the coachman said. He pulled on his white wig, making it all crooked.

"It'll do. It'll do," said Mrs. Merryball.

"Life is but a dream. . . ." Now the Fairy Godmother pointed at the kids playing video games by the soda machines. *Poof! Poof! Poof! Poof!* There were four scruffy-looking horses to pull the coach.

"It'll do. It'll do," Mrs. Merryball said to Cinderella, patting her shoulder.

"Now for the footman. Hmmmm. The footman. The footman." Mrs. Merryball pointed her wand all around the alley. Finally she dropped her arms. "Oh, dear. I seem to be stuck on the footman."

Now this was something that Fiona and Frieda had always wondered about.

"Um, what's a footman?" Fiona asked.

"Why, he's the one who opens the coach's door," the Fairy Godmother said. "Row, row, row—," she started singing again.

"Are you kidding me?!" Cinderella must have temporarily forgotten she was a maiden, because she got really rude for a second and screamed, "I can open my *own* door!"

"Oh, yes, quite," the Fairy Godmother said. "I suppose any girl who can zip a zipper can pull a handle. . . . That leaves just one last thing."

Then with a quick wand flip, she put Cinderella in a big, white, ruffly, puffy, ribbony, lacy dress.

Cinderella stood there for a minute looking like a depressed wedding cake. Then her chin wrinkled and she started to cry.

Sniff. Oooooh. Hiccup. Waaaaaah!

"My dear, my dear, what is wrong?" Mrs. Merryball wasn't exactly the most on-the-ball Fairy Godmother. But in her defense, she really did seem worried about Cinderella.

"My dress!" Cinderella wailed.

"Oh, I see," Mrs. Merryball said. "I forgot a sash and a train. Of course, just one second—"

Cinderella cried even harder.

"Excuse me, Mrs. Merryball," Fiona interrupted. "What Cinderella is trying to explain, I believe, is that she would prefer her own dress. The one she made herself out of shells and rainbow light and stuff."

"Of course!" Mrs. Merryball said. "How silly of me." *Poof!*

In movies when something really amazing happens, they do this thing that sounds like angels singing or light streams through clouds. Or everything gets white and fuzzy and moves in slow motion. Well, *all* those things happened when Cinderella stood there in her own dress. It was like a fairy tale—really.

When the angels stopped singing, Mrs. Merryball looked down at Cinderella's feet. She was still wearing Fiona's bowling shoes.

The Fairy Godmother clicked her tongue. "Those won't do, won't do one bit." *Poof!* And that's how Cinderella got real glass slippers to wear to the ball.

The coach was ready. The horses were ready. The coachman was ready. Cinderella was ready.

"Now, remember dear," Mrs. Merryball said to Cinderella. "You must leave the ball by midnight. At the stroke of 12, the spell will be broken and all will be as it was before."

By now, Cinderella was way too happy to care about details. But Frieda was never too anything to not care about details. Quickly, she undid her digital watch. She programmed the alarm for 11:55.

"*Pssst.* Cinderella, take this," she said, handing the watch to the maiden.

"Thank you!" Cinderella said. She shoved the watch behind one of the feathers in her dress (otherwise it would have ruined her outfit).

"What a great idea, Frieda. Now I don't have to worry about a thing."

Famous last words.

Chapter 6

Fiona and Frieda opened the bowling alley's double doors, and the coach sped off to the ball.

"Good-bye, dears," Mrs. Merryball said, packing up her wand. "Do come visit me for some zucchini bread sometime." She waved and walked down the block toward Castle Apartments.

Fiona just stood there. Frieda just stood there. Then they looked at each other for a second before they both started screaming and jumping up and down.

"*Whooo-hoooo!*" Fiona shouted. "Can you believe it? We met Cinderella!"

"And the mean stepsisters!" Frieda said.

"And we saved the day!" Fiona said. "Now all Cinderella has to do is go to the ball and have the prince fall in love with her."

The two girls started acting out the scene they had acted out so many times before. Fiona was Cinderella, of course, and Frieda was in such a good mood she didn't mind being the prince. Plus, she got to do special effects.

"Oh, my darling, you look so beautiful," Frieda said, kissing Fiona's hand.

"My prince, you look good, too," Fiona said.

"La-da-dee-da," the girls sang and waltzed around the bowling alley.

Everything was going along well until Frieda realized something. Something awful. They had gotten to the end of the ball, the part where Frieda was supposed to say *"bong, bong, bong"* as the clock struck 12. This was the part where Cinderella was supposed to run down the steps in a hurry. Where she left one glass slipper—the slipper that fit only her foot. The slipper that the prince used to find the princess. The slipper that saves the day.

But Frieda had given Cinderella the watch with the alarm. That meant no hurry. No glass slipper on the stairs. No way for the prince to ever, ever find her.

Fiona noticed that all of a sudden Frieda looked like she'd just taken a bite of poison apple.

"What's wrong?" Fiona asked her friend.

Frieda could barely explain it all without crying.

"It's okay," Fiona said. She hugged Frieda. "It's okay. I have a plan."

Frieda was feeling so bad that Fiona didn't want to tell her right away. Fiona's plan was to go to the ball and get the watch back. Fiona reasoned, sometimes the simplest plans are best.

Of course, the girls had no idea where the ball was and that meant—

"Mrs. Merryball! Mrs. Merryball!"

The girls caught up with the Fairy Godmother in the lobby of Castle Apartments. They spotted her in the elevator just as the doors closed.

"The stairs!" Fiona shouted.

"Faster, faster," Frieda panted, all the way up eight flights of stairs and down the hall. Finally, they reached number 803.

"Mrs. Merryball!" Frieda pounded on the door and Fiona rung the bell. "Mrs. Merryball! Please, open up!"

"Just one minute!" Mrs. Merryball called out. Then pots clanged and something splatted.

Mrs. Merryball was whistling "Jingle Bells" as she opened the door. She was wearing oven mitts and an apron with zucchini stuffed in the pockets.

"Fiona, Frieda," she said. "How lovely to see you. When I saw you coming, I thought I'd better get started on some zippy, zingy zucchini bread."

"Sorry, Mrs. Merryball," Frieda said. "But we we need to see Cinderella right away."

"Oh, yes, of course, the whole watch problem," the Fairy Godmother said.

"How do *you* know about that?" Frieda asked. Mrs. Merryball pointed to her *250 years old and still cookin'!* apron.

"Did you forget who I am?" Mrs. Merryball asked, winking.

"Uh, right. So, where is she?" Frieda asked. She was chewing on her hair now.

"Why, at the ball, dear."

"Yes, yes. But *where* is the ball?" Frieda said, through a big wad of overgrown bangs.

"Why, at the king's home, of course."

"And where is *that?*" If Frieda were a cartoon character, there would have been smoke coming out of her ears.

"Well, I believe the Kinglymans live in the penthouse apartment. Top floor."

"You mean the ball is *here*? At Castle Apartments?" Frieda asked.

"Why, where else would it be?" Mrs. Merryball seemed even more confused than usual.

"Let's go!" Fiona said, grabbing Frieda's arm.

"Oh, dears, aren't you forgetting something?" Mrs. Merryball asked. "Here, do allow me."

"Row, row, row . . ." *Poof!* Fiona looked down in amazement. She was wearing a light blue gown with pearl buttons and lace gloves that went up past her elbows.

"Your boat, gently down the . . ." *Poof!* Frieda got a—bunny suit?

"Whoops. Sorry!" Mrs. Merryball giggled.

Poof! Poof!

There stood Frieda, dazzling in a shimmery black gown with a red, furry shawl and a diamond necklace that dangled almost to her belly button.

"You look like Cruella De Vil!" Fiona said to her friend.

"And you look like Cinderella!" Frieda said. The girls spun around to see how far their skirts flared out.

"Can I try on your gloves?" Frieda asked Fiona.

"Can I try on your shawl?" Fiona asked Frieda.

"No time for that, girls. Off you go!" Mrs. Merryball said. "It's almost midnight at the ball."

"What? How can that be?" Frieda said. It had only felt like five minutes.

"Well, remember, time flies when you're having fun. And Cinderella's having a ball!"

Fiona and Frieda looked at each other and giggled. Then, they hurried back to the elevator.

Chapter 7

When Fiona and Frieda arrived at the penthouse apartment, it was empty. The girls could hear violin music playing on the roof. They climbed the stairs to the rooftop. Then they stood in the doorway, too amazed to move.

For there, at the king's ball, was every princess, prince, witch, queen, king, dwarf, wolf, and fairy that they had ever read about. Snow White was sipping orange juice with her ruby red lips. Rapunzel had her hair in a bun the size of beach ball. Prince what's-his-name from Sleeping Beauty was pacing nearby.

The girls could have stood there forever, but then Frieda remembered the whole Cinderella fairy tale was about to be ruined because of her.

"C'mon, let's find her!" Frieda said.

The girls slipped into the crowd. They squeezed their way through a group of dwarfs playing miniature golf. They looked behind an apple stand with a weird Free Apples for Princesses sign. They even looked in the Beast's magic mirror. But no Cinderella.

Where was she?

Fiona looked at the clock. 11:55! She swung around. "Look!" she shouted to Frieda. There was the back of Cinderella's dress slipping through the door. "Let's go get her!"

The girls ran out the door and down the stairs to the elevator, but the doors were just closing. "Faster, faster!" Frieda panted all the way down ten flights of stairs until—at last— they caught up with Cinderella just as she was stepping out of the elevator into the lobby.

"Oh, Fiona! Frieda!" Cinderella skipped toward them. "I had such a lovely, lovely time. I met the prince and we danced and my mean stepsisters didn't even recognize me and—"

"Did you tell him your name by any chance?" Frieda interrupted hopefully.

"Oh, now that you mention it, I must have forgotten," Cinderella said. "And then when my alarm went off he was in the bathroom, so I didn't even get a chance to say good-bye. I do hope he doesn't think I'm terribly rude."

"Come on, Cinderella," Frieda said, plucking the watch out of Cinderella's dress. "We *have* to go back upstairs. You *have* to leave the ball one more time."

Cinderella was probably really confused, but Frieda had this way of talking where you didn't ask questions. So, Cinderella followed Frieda and Fiona back into the elevator.

Bong! Bong! Bong!

"What's that noise?" Cinderella said as they stepped out onto the tenth floor.

"It's the clock striking midnight," Frieda said. "Come on!" She led Cinderella up the stairs.

Bong! Bong! Bong!

"The bongs—they're too fast!" Fiona shouted.

Bong! Bong!

The bongs rang out as fast as beads spilling on a floor. By the eighth bong, Frieda realized an immediate backup plan was necessary.

Bong!

Frieda grabbed Cinderella's foot.

Bong!

She took off the glass slipper.

Bong!

She wound up her bowling arm and chucked the shoe up the stairs as hard as she could. The glass slipper sailed through the air.

Bong!

The twelfth bong and—*poof!* Fiona and Frieda watched in horror. Cinderella instantly transformed back into her bowling disguise. And the glass slipper turned back into a bowling shoe. It landed with a thud on the top step.

"That's not supposed to happen!" Fiona shrieked.

But Frieda just shook her head, "I always said that part didn't make sense."

"Come on! Come on! The prince is going to see you. We've *got* to get out of here!" Fiona tugged at Cinderella's sleeve.

Chapter 8

Cinderella had reached her confusion limit. She refused to even budge. "We can't just leave your shoe there, Fiona," she said. "How are you going to bowl in your club with only one shoe?"

Fiona got all teary-eyed and choked up like an old lady at a wedding at what happened next. Cinderella did something really and truly worthy of a fairy-tale princess. She decided it was more important to get her friend's shoe than to keep the prince from seeing her in ugly clothes.

Cinderella climbed up the stairs. When she bent down to pick up the shoe, another hand grabbed at it from above. The prince was standing on the step with Cinderella, holding Fiona's bowling shoe.

"Oh, hi!" he said. His face lit up like a glow-in-the-dark yo-yo when he saw Cinderella. "I was wondering where you went."

(Obviously, he was a lot smarter than the stepsisters, because he recognized her instantly in her bowling disguise.)

"Oh, please excuse my rudeness," Cinderella said. "I had someplace I needed to go right away."

The prince looked at the pink and black bowling shirt. He looked at the bowling shoe.

"To the bowling alley?" he asked.

"Actually yes."

"Cool! I love bowling."

"I'm a little new to it myself," Cinderella said. "But I'd love to practice. Shall we roll a game?"

"Sure! I'm Ashford by the way," the prince said, handing Cinderella her bowling shoe.

"I know. I'm Cinderella."

Ashford looked at her shirt again and noticed that *Fiona* was written across the pocket. He asked, "Then who's Fiona?"

"There she is," Cinderella said. "These are my two wonderful friends, Fiona and Frieda." Fiona gave her own Prince Charming grin. Frieda got all shy and just waved a little.

"So, um, why are you wearing Fiona's shirt?" the prince asked.

"It's a long story," Cinderella said. "I'll tell you all about it while we bowl."

At that, Fiona, Frieda, Cinderella, and Ashford left the ball to go bowling at Moonlight Lanes.

On their way out of Castle Apartments, Cinderella picked up the red, pearly-swirly bowling ball that was sitting on the sidewalk.

"I'll use this ball. I bet it's lucky," she said, winking at Fiona and Frieda.

At Moonlight Lanes, the video-game kids and the shoe-rental guy were already back doing their own thing.

At this point, Fiona and Frieda realized they'd better leave Cinderella and the prince to themselves. They decided to roll their own game instead. There was just one more red, pearly-swirly bowling ball left in the whole place. Both girls spotted it at the exact same time.

"Look, Fiona, a—"

"Look, Frieda, a—"

Frieda was going to say, "a swirly red bowling ball." Fiona was going to say, "a pearly red bowling ball." But the girls never got a chance to finish. Frieda said "swirly" at the exact moment Fiona said "pearly" and—

There was that fluffy magic stuff in the air again.

"It must have been the rhyme!" Fiona said.

"We're magic rhymers!" Frieda exclaimed.

For there they were, back at the curly blue slide. This time they could hear everything. Only ten minutes had gone by! It was almost time for everyone to go back inside the school.

"I guess Mrs. Merryball was right," Fiona said.

"Time does fly when you're at a ball," Frieda said.

Fiona giggled. Frieda giggled. Then Frieda decided they'd better test their magic rhyming powers. They each agreed on what to say.

"One, two, three," they counted.

"Jelly beans!" Fiona said as Frieda chimed in with, "Smelly jeans!"

Just as the magic stuff cleared away, they saw the Big Bad Wolf zoom by on roller skates.

As for Cinderella, well, she turned out to be a natural bowler. Soon the prince and Cinderella joined the same bowling league. One night, the prince proposed to Cinderella by writing, "Will you marry me?" on her lucky bowling ball. She said yes, of course!

The prince and Cinderella were married during a rooftop ball at Castle Apartments.

Mrs. Merryball made a zucchini bread wedding cake. Fiona wore her blue dress with Frieda's furry red shawl, and Frieda wore her black dress with Fiona's lace gloves. Even the mean stepsisters showed up, though they had to leave early after a fight that ended in the pool.

And that is the story of how Cinderella and Prince Ashford lived happily ever after.

#3. Swirly...

Pearly...

#1. Eye of frog,
Enchanted hog,
Magic willow,
Flying pillow

#2. A sneezing chum,
A stick of gum,
A grand to-do,
No boo-hoo—
... Achoo!

#4. Jelly beans,
smelly jeans!